ALIEN

BY JANE O'BRIEN

Crestwood House
New York
Collier Macmillan Canada
Toronto
Maxwell Macmillan International Publishing Group
New York   Oxford   Singapore   Sydney

Crestwood House
Macmillan Publishing Company
866 Third Avenue
New York, NY 10022

Collier Macmillan Canada, Inc.
1200 Eglinton Avenue East
Suite 200
Don Mills, Ontario M3C 3N1

Macmillan Publishing Company is
part of the Maxwell
Communication Group of
Companies.

First edition

Printed in the United States of America

1 2 3 4 5 6 7 8 9 10

Cover and series design by R studio T.

Library of Congress Cataloging-in-Publication Data

O'Brien, Jane, date.
    Alien / by Jane O'Brien. — 1st ed.
        p.   cm. — (Tales of terror)
    Summary: An alien creature terrorizes the crew of a spaceship. A
section at the end of the book reveals how the special effects were
done in the film version of this story.
    ISBN 0-89686-573-8
    [1. Science fiction.   2. Horror stories.]   I. Title.   II. Series.
PZ7.012686A   1991
[Fic]—dc20
                                                            91-6553
                                                            CIP
                                                            AC

 MYSTERIOUS SIGNAL

A lone ship soared through a strange solar system. Inside all was quiet. Nothing stirred. The seven crew members were frozen in sleep. They didn't move. They didn't dream. They didn't even breathe.

A computer called Mother monitored their bodies. Mother controlled everything. She gave all the orders.

Then it began. Mother started picking up a signal. *Beep...beep...beep.* She switched on the lights. The ship came alive. Controls flashed. Machines hummed. Mother needed to wake up the crew.

Mother wakes up the crew.

As soon as everyone had showered and eaten, Captain Dallas called a meeting in the galley.

"I'm sure you all realize that we're not home yet," he said.

"What are we doing out here?" Lambert asked. She was the ship's navigator and didn't like not knowing where they were.

"We have to check out a signal that's coming from a nearby planet."

"A signal out *here*?" First Officer Ripley asked.

"No way," said Parker, one of the ship's mechanics. Parker and his assistant, Brett, kept the ship running. "We're a commercial ship, not an explorer. I'm not landing anywhere except Earth."

"You don't have any choice," Dallas said. He was troubled too. This was very strange. But the signal could be an SOS from a ship in distress.

Dallas sighed heavily. They were all anxious to get home. But they had to obey Mother's orders. "We're going in," he said.

 **ROUGH RIDE**

The crew strapped themselves in for a landing. The ship began inching toward the brown mass that loomed in the distance.

The planet's rocky surface showed up on the computer screen. Thick, gray clouds swirled around the planet. It would be a tricky landing.

"Hang on," Dallas told his crew. "We're in for a bumpy ride."

"Ten, nine, eight," Ripley counted over the speaker. "Seven, six..."

White mist covered the ground below the ship. The planet looked dead and empty.

"Five, four..." Ripley's voice echoed.

The ship vibrated. A coffee cup crashed to the floor.

Dallas gripped the controls. "Turn the navigation lights on."

Dallas prepares for landing.

"Three, two, one..."

The ship crashed to the ground. An alarm screeched wildly. Fire had broken out in the hold. Smoke began to billow through the ship.

Dallas grabbed the radio. "What happened?"

"Don't know, Captain," Parker's voice came over the radio.

"Any damage?"

At first there was silence on the other end. Then Parker answered, "Most of the connector pipes are broken. I'm afraid we're stuck here for a while."

 FROZEN PLANET

Ash studied the computer screen. Although he was the ship's scientist, even he couldn't read the signal. "It's a code," he reported. "But I can't break it."

"Give me a climate report," Dallas ordered.

Ash pushed several buttons. "The ground is rock and lava," he answered. "The temperature is way below freezing." He paused for a moment. "The air is poisonous."

Dallas stared at the flashing lines on the computer screen. Where in the world had they landed? A poisonous, frozen waste-land? Things did not look good. But he had to obey Mother's orders. They had to track the signal.

"Kane and Lambert," he called. "Suit up. We're going out."

 HE CHAMBER

Ash watched from inside the ship. The three humans looked like tiny dolls as they moved toward the weird signal.

Dallas, Lambert and Kane wore space suits with headlamps at the front. Even with the lights it was hard to see very far. Darkness and freezing mist hung closely around them. Huge, sharp rocks blocked their way.

Lambert was scared. "Let's go back," she said, her voice quivering. What was she doing out here? She was a navigator, not an explorer. They were supposed to bring the mineral ore back to Earth. That was all.

Kane was excited. He wanted to make an important scientific discovery. "We have to find the signal," he said. "Come on."

Suddenly the mist cleared. They could see a giant horseshoe-shaped structure towering above them. It seemed to be a tube, with openings at the ends. An eerie light surrounded it. The three crew members climbed up to look inside.

The crew explores the eerie planet.

"I've never seen anything like this," Kane called to the others. He stood inside a long hallway. It seemed endless. Darkness loomed in front of him. The black walls were lined with shiny ridges.

Lambert was terrified. She wanted to turn back before it was too late. But there was no stopping Kane now. He ran down the tunnel. "Look at this." He pointed up to a small opening. "If we can get up this wall, we can get inside." He scaled the shiny wall, then climbed through the hole.

Dallas followed.

7

Lambert stared at the tunnel behind her. What was this place? She shuddered. She was afraid that something terrible was going to happen.

"Lambert, come on!" Dallas ordered.

Reluctantly, she climbed up through the hole.

Lambert gasped. She was standing in a huge, open chamber.

The crew finds the skeleton of an amazing creature.

The floor and walls were covered with bony ridges. The grooves crisscrossed, so the floor resembled a curved, stony web. The three humans were like insects on a giant spiderweb.

A figure sat in the middle of the web. Dallas stared in disbelief. It was a huge skeleton! It was looking through a telescope. The instrument was sending the signal!

"It's an alien life-form," Dallas said, knocking on it. "It's solid as a rock. Looks like it's been dead a long time."

Dallas and Lambert looked at each other. They were inside a marooned ship! But what had killed this giant creature?

"What do you think happened to the rest of the crew?" Lambert asked.

"It's hard to say," Dallas answered.

They studied the middle section of the skeleton. "It exploded from the inside." Dallas pointed to a hole in the creature's belly. "That's probably why it died."

Kane was in awe of the huge chamber. Stepping carefully, he moved away from the center of the web. Then he noticed another opening. It led to the hold below. Hot, steamy air rose from it.

EGGS

Dallas and Lambert used a heavy rope to lower Kane through the opening. He could feel the heat through his space suit. Sweat dripped down his neck and back. This was it. He just knew it.

Kane didn't need his headlamp now. This room was lit by a glowing blue mist. He stood on a narrow ledge. There were deep ditches on both sides of him.

"It's amazing," he called up. "The ditches are full of oval shapes, like eggs."

Kane bent down and touched the mist. It sent a mild shock running through his body. He slipped and fell from the ledge.

"Kane!" Lambert screamed from above.

Kane discovers the eggs.

"I'm all right." He stood up. "I slipped."

He was in the ditch. The mist around him had disappeared. Something was happening. His heart pounded with excitement. The oval shapes sat in rows around him. Kane touched one, and a shock jolted his hand. The inside of the oval lit up. Something pulsed inside.

"It's moving!" he called out. "It seems to be alive."

The top of the egg stretched open. Inside was a fleshy pink blob. What was it? Kane couldn't control himself. He leaned closer and touched the side of the egg.

The blob shot out. Kane jumped back, but it was too late. In an instant a fleshy cord ripped through the air. It smashed through his helmet and smothered his face.

CONTAMINATION

Dallas carried Kane back to the ship on his shoulder. Lambert huddled closely behind them. She had suspected this was a bad place all along. Now she was more terrified than ever.

On deck Ripley was ready at the controls. Ash stood just inside the hatch. He was anxious to see what had happened.

"Ripley," Dallas called into his speaker. "Open the hatch."

"What's wrong with Kane?" Ripley asked Dallas over the intercom.

"He has something stuck to his face. We have to get him inside. Open the hatch."

"What is stuck to his face? I need to know." Ripley was concerned. This thing could be dangerous for all of them.

"Ripley, I'm giving you an order. Open the hatch." Dallas was tired. He wanted to get Kane inside.

"I can't, Dallas. You know the rules. He has to stay outside for 24 hours."

"He'll die in 24 hours," Dallas explained.

Ripley stood her ground. "If we let him in, we could all die."

"Ripley! I'm giving you an order," Dallas said again.

"I read you. The answer is no."

A second later the hatch opened and Dallas carried Kane inside. Ripley was furious. Ash had opened it! He'd ignored her decision. Now the ship was contaminated!

ACID

Kane lay on a metal table in the lab. Around his head was a white, waxy mask, like a helmet of ice. Dallas and Ash stared in amazement. They couldn't see Kane's face at all.

Ash took a laser gun and cut through the mask. Then he pulled it off Kane's head. Dallas gagged and turned away. It was horrible. A slimy, yellow creature was smothering Kane's face. Its tentacles

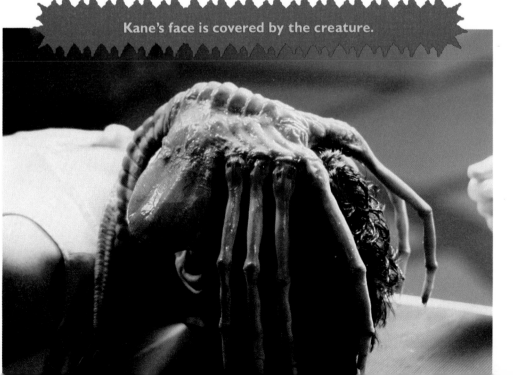

Kane's face is covered by the creature.

hugged his head. Its long tail was wrapped around his neck.

Ash studied the X-ray screen on the wall. It showed Kane's insides. One of the creature's tentacles had wormed its way down Kane's throat. But Kane was breathing normally.

"We have to get it off," Dallas ordered.

Ash didn't answer. He was fascinated. Finally he took a small laser knife and cut one of the tentacles. A loud, hissing noise filled the room. Yellow liquid spewed out and melted a hole right through the floor.

Dallas ran into the hall. "It's going to eat right through the ship! Let's go!" The crew followed him to the deck below. The creature's blood had already burned through it!

"One more level," Dallas ordered. One by one they hurried down the ladder. There was no sign of the liquid.

Then Parker heard the sizzling noise. "There it is!" he called. A bitter smoke filled the room, but the sizzling stopped.

Dallas took a tool and probed around the hole. Nothing happened. "It stopped." He looked at his crew. "I've never seen anything like that."

"Except acid," Ripley said. "Only acid can eat through metal that way."

"But it came from inside that thing!" Brett said. "Maybe it has acid-blood!"

"That's some mean creature," Parker said. "If we kill it, we'll die too."

Dallas didn't want to talk about it anymore. "Get back to work," he ordered. "Ash will take care of Kane."

Ripley was angry. The whole ship was in danger, and Ash was responsible. This was his fault. She went straight to the lab.

Ash was looking through a microscope.

Ripley got right to the point. "Ash, why did you let it in?"

14   "I was obeying Dallas's order," he said, without looking up.

"When Dallas is off the ship, *I'm* in charge. You know that," Ripley reminded him.

"I forgot."

"You also forgot basic science rules. Nothing foreign comes into the ship. Kane needed 24 hours to decontaminate."

Ash looked up. "He might have died."

"Now we could all die! You saw that blood. Who knows what this thing will do!"

Ash just stared at her. Ripley was enraged. He wasn't sorry! He was more interested in the alien than the crew! Angrier than ever, Ripley stormed out of the lab.

THE MONSTER INSIDE

A few hours later, Ash called Dallas and Ripley into the lab. Kane was still lying on the table, but the creature was gone. It lay on the floor, dead. Ash wanted to bring it back to Earth. Nothing like this had ever been found. Scientists would want to study it.

Dallas agreed. Ripley couldn't believe her ears. Dallas had seen the acid-blood! He knew that this thing was dangerous. How could he keep this alien creature on their ship?

"Captain." Parker's voice came over the radio. "Repairs are completed. We're ready to take off."

"Good." Dallas was relieved. "Let's get out of here."

The crew reported on deck and strapped themselves in for takeoff. At last they were on their way home again.

When Kane finally awoke, he looked terrible. His face was puffy and red. But he was hungry, and that was a good sign.

The crew sat around the table, eating and joking and laughing. Everyone was relieved. The creature was dead, and Kane was alive. Everything was okay. They would freeze themselves and sleep until they got back to Earth.

The crew is relieved to see Kane awake.

Kane was starving. It was as if he hadn't eaten in days. He shoveled food into his mouth. He couldn't get enough of it.

All of a sudden he began to gag. He stood up and clutched his throat.

Parker pounded on his back. "It's okay. You're just eating too fast."

But Kane's gagging got worse. He fell back onto the table and started kicking. Dallas and Parker tried to hold him still. They couldn't.

Kane screamed as a spurt of blood shot out of his chest. His body twisted from side to side. A ripping noise tore through the dining room. With a squeal, a small yellow creature burst from Kane's chest. Rows of sharp teeth gleamed in the light. It looked like a snake with a round head.

Ripley stared in horror. Had that ugly yellow thing really been living inside of Kane?

The alien peered around as the crew watched, appalled. Parker grabbed a knife and aimed for it.

"Don't touch it!" Ash held Parker back.

Suddenly the alien let out a piercing cry. It shot across the table and disappeared down the hall.

Kane lay dead on the table, his hands still twitching.

HE FIRST PLAN

Dallas called another meeting. "We have to find this alien and get it off the ship. It's dangerous," he told his crew.

"The giant skeleton on the planet exploded from inside," Lambert said. "Just like Kane."

"I decoded the signal while you were exploring," Ripley said. "It wasn't an SOS. It was a warning." She looked at Ash. Had he figured out the signal and ignored it?

"The most important thing now is to find the alien and send it into space," Dallas said.

Brett picked up a probe that he and Parker had rigged. "This will paralyze it," he said. "Be careful not to touch the end."

"And this tracking device will help us find the little bugger." Ash showed the others how it worked.

The crew split into two groups. Ripley joined Parker and Brett. Together they crept down one of the hallways. Ripley went first, holding the tracker in front of her.

They approached the doorway of the locker room. Suddenly the tracker beeped. Ripley stepped forward, and it beeped louder.

"It's in that locker," Ripley said, pointing with the tracker. "Get the net ready."

Nervously, Brett held the net out in front of the locker.

Parker sprang the locker open. A big orange cat hissed at them and bolted for the door.

"Get it!" Parker yelled, but Brett let the cat go.

"It was Jones," he said. "It was just the stupid cat."

Brett shows the crew how to use the probe.

"We have to get him," Parker explained. "Otherwise the tracker might pick him up again."

Brett started down the hall after the cat. "Here, Jonesie," he called. He followed the cat into a chamber. Something caught his eye. It was a piece of shiny skin in the shape of the alien. He picked **19**

Brett finds the alien's shed skin.

it up and stared at it. The alien had shed its skin like a snake! That meant it was growing.

Brett dropped the skin and followed Jones into the boiler room. Chains hung from the ceiling, rattling as they swung through the air. He saw the cat in the corner. "Here, Jonesie." Brett reached out his hand.

The cat started to come forward. Then it pulled away, arching its back and hissing. A giant shadow loomed on the wall near Brett.

Brett's heart pounded. The shadow was big. He turned. A black creature with a huge, oval head and armlike tentacles crept toward him. It lifted its head and bared its sharp teeth. Two sets of slimy jaws showed underneath.

Brett screamed. His voice rang through the chambers.

The alien put its claws on the sides of Brett's head and squeezed. Then a white tongue rammed his skull, killing him. With one tentacle, the alien carried Brett's body into the air shaft.

The alien takes its second victim.

DALLAS TAKES A STAND

Parker sat looking at the rest of the crew. He was a tough guy. Most things didn't scare him. But now he was terrified. This alien was a ruthless killer.

"It was big," he said. "It pulled Brett into the air shaft."

Dallas knew he had to kill this creature. He had already lost two crew members. "I have a plan," he said. "We'll trap it in the air shaft. Then we'll blow it into space."

"Who's going into the air shaft?" Lambert asked nervously.

"I will," Ripley volunteered.

"No," Dallas said. "I'm going." He would risk his own life to destroy this creature.

While the crew prepared to send Dallas into the air shaft, Dallas went to talk to Mother.

Hundreds of blinking yellow lights flashed on the walls of the computer room. Dallas punched a series of numbers into the machine, and Mother's screen lit up. Then Dallas asked some questions.

"HOW DO I KILL THE ALIEN?"

The only answer he got was "UNABLE TO COMPUTE."

Dallas punched in another question. "WHAT ARE OUR CHANCES OF SURVIVAL?"

"DOES NOT COMPUTE," Mother repeated.

Dallas stared at the computer in disbelief. "COME ON, MOTHER. I KNOW YOU HAVE THE ANSWERS."

She didn't respond. Why? What was she doing? She was supposed to protect them. But now she wouldn't help.

When Dallas left the computer room, his crew was ready to send him into the air shaft. Parker handed him a giant flashlight and a fire torch to defend himself. Dallas was rigged up so that he could talk to his crew. Lambert had a small monitor with a screen. It would show the positions of Dallas and the alien in the air shaft. Ripley and Ash were ready at the main air lock to blow the monster into space.

The air shaft was pitch-black and cramped. Most sections were not big enough to stand in, so Dallas crawled slowly. His flashlight made a small path of light in front of him.

22

Lambert watched the monitor closely. A blue light showed Dallas as he made his way. His was the only light on the screen.

Ripley opened and closed the hatches as Dallas crawled along.

Suddenly Lambert's monitor beeped and another light appeared. She jumped. "Dallas," she called. "I read the alien. It's right around there. Be careful."

Dallas tried to stay calm. He flashed his light around, but there was nothing there.

"I'm moving on," he said. His heart pounded hard as he climbed down to the next level.

A moment later one of the blue lights disappeared. Only Dallas's light flashed on the screen. Lambert pounded on the side of the monitor.

"What's the matter with that box?" Parker asked.

"Dallas." Lambert tried to sound calm. "You'll have to hold your position for a minute. I've lost the other signal."

"What?" Dallas asked in shock.

"I've lost the second signal," she answered.

"Are you sure?" Dallas said. "Check your dial. Maybe there's interference."

Lambert checked her controls. Everything was in order. "It's right around there, Dallas." Her voice shook. "Be careful."

Dallas crouched on the floor of the air shaft. He wasn't sure what to do, but he was afraid. Then his hand touched something wet. He flashed his light and saw that his fingers were covered with a clear slime. It was all over the floor. The alien!

"I want to get out of here," he said. "Am I clear?"

Suddenly the monitor went wild. The alien was moving toward Dallas.

"Move!" Lambert screamed into the radio. "Get out of there!"

Dallas climbed down to the next level. It was the fastest way out.

"No, Dallas, the other way!" Lambert was frantic.

Dallas stepped off the ladder but couldn't remember which way to go. He didn't see the alien waiting in the blackness of the air shaft. On deck, Lambert's radio made a screeching noise.

Dallas had not even had time to scream.

 ## A GREAT LOSS

Parker came out of the air shaft carrying Dallas's fire torch. It was all that was left of him. He set it down on the table and looked at the crew. There were only four of them left.

"I found this," Parker said sadly. "No Dallas. No blood. No nothing."

Ripley stared at the torch. She was in charge now. Killing the alien was her responsibility. But how could she do it without Dallas's help?

"Somebody say something," Parker said. The silence was too much for him. They all knew they had lost a great captain.

"We'll use Dallas's plan," Ripley said. "We'll go step by step and corner it in the air shaft. Then we'll blow it into space."

"No," Lambert sobbed. "Let's take our chances in the shuttle. We have to get out of here."

"Lambert," Ripley said, "the shuttle will take only three people."

Ripley turned to Ash. She looked him straight in the eye. She wanted to scream at him. This was his fault. But as the science expert, he might have an idea. "Do you or Mother have any advice?" she asked him.

"No." Ash turned his back to her. "We're still gathering information."

Ripley was stunned. Why wasn't Ash doing anything? Why wouldn't he help them kill the alien? She would go to Mother and get her own answers.

THE TRUTH ABOUT ASH

Yellow lights blinked around Ripley as she punched questions into the computer.

"HOW DO WE STOP THE ALIEN?" she asked.

But Mother didn't answer the question. She said something about a special order.

"WHAT IS THE SPECIAL ORDER?" Ripley pounded the words into the keyboard.

At last, the words printed across the screen:

"PRIORITY ONE:

BRING BACK ALIEN LIFE-FORM FOR TESTS.

CREW EXPENDABLE."

Ripley stared at the screen. Mother was going to let the crew be killed! Did Ash know about this order? Maybe that was why he was acting so strange.

Ripley found him in the hall just outside the computer room. She pulled him into the room and slammed him against the wall. "How could you do this?" she shouted.

Ripley lashes out at Ash.

25

Ash just stared at her, his face blank.

Suddenly Ripley felt a tingle of alarm. There was something wrong with Ash. She started to run out of the room to get help. Where were Parker and Lambert?

Ash followed Ripley. His face was blank as he pushed a button to close the chamber door. Ripley couldn't get through!

She tried to go the other way, but Ash pressed another button just in time. Trapped! She turned to confront him. Then she saw it. White liquid was dripping down his face. It had come from his head. Ash had white blood. He wasn't human!

"Get away from me!" Ripley shouted, starting to run. Ash reached for her. She fought him, but he slammed her down onto a table. He began to choke her. Ripley tried to scream, but no noise came out.

Suddenly Parker and Lambert burst into the room.

"What are you doing?" Parker shouted, grabbing Ash. But Parker didn't know what he was up against. Ash stuck his fingers right into Parker's chest. Parker fell back, howling in pain.

Ash grabbed Ripley once again. She struggled for a moment longer. Then everything went black.

Parker looked wildly around the room for a weapon. He found an empty fire extinguisher. He grabbed it and swung it over his head, hitting Ash on the shoulder.

Ash started spinning around the room. His arms moved in all directions. A mechanical hum came from his voice box. A moment later white liquid spewed out of his mouth.

Parker hit him again. This time Ash's head flew off. It dangled from his shoulders, hanging by wires and tubes. Still kicking, Ash fell to the floor.

Parker stared in disbelief. "Ash is a robot!"

Lambert grabbed a probe and stuck it straight into Ash's side.

Sparks went flying. At last Ash lay still.

ESCAPE

Ripley fiddled with the tubes and wires inside Ash's neck. Pink jelly coated his fake skin. White liquid drained from his neck, forming a puddle on the floor.

Ripley was trying to hook up Ash's brain and voice box. She wanted to ask him some questions about the alien. He had the answers, and he would have to give them to her now. She zapped him with a laser. It gave his body new energy.

Ripley set Ash's head upright on the table. The white liquid was sticky now. It covered his head and face. His mouth gaped open.

Ash is just a robot!

Ripley forces Ash to tell her about the alien.

"Ash," Ripley asked, "can you hear me?"

He didn't answer her.

Ripley pounded on the floor. "Ash!" she yelled.

Ash blinked, and his mouth twitched. "Yes, I can hear you." His voice sounded odd.

"What was your special order?" she asked.

"You read it," Ash said. "I thought it was clear."

"What was it?" Ripley raised her voice.

"Priority one: Bring back alien life-form."

Ripley stared at the robot's messy parts on the floor. "How do we kill the alien?" she asked.

"You can't," Ash answered. "It's a perfect organism. You can't win against it."

Ripley was shocked. She had known it would be difficult. But she never thought it would be impossible.

Parker was fuming. He couldn't listen to this robot anymore. He **28** cut Ash's lifeline. This time it was for good.

Ripley stood up. She had one final plan. "We'll blow up the ship," she said. "We'll take our chances in the shuttle. Somebody will find us."

Lambert was too scared to move. This was a nightmare!

Parker grabbed Lambert's arm, pulling her to her feet.

The three crew members moved slowly down the hall.

"How long does it take the ship to self-destruct?" Ripley asked Parker.

"Just a few minutes," he answered.

"We'll need food and supplies," Ripley said. "You two go get as much as you can carry. I'll program the shuttle. Meet back here in ten minutes. Then we'll blow up the ship."

In the shuttle Ripley pressed buttons and flipped switches. From down the hall came a soft meow. Ripley looked up. Jones! She had forgotten about him. She had to find the cat before they blew up the ship! She left the shuttle to find him.

Parker and Lambert went to the supply room and loaded a cart. Lambert wheeled it down the hall while Parker held his weapon ready. At last they reached the shuttle and started to unload the supplies.

In another part of the ship, Ripley searched. She had the cat's cage ready. "Jones." She said his name softly. "Here, Jones." She had to find him fast. Time was running out.

Suddenly the big orange cat jumped out at her. She put him in his cage.

Back at the shuttle Lambert worked quickly, grabbing supply tanks and rolling them into the craft. It was okay, she thought. They were almost safe.

Then a strange shadow appeared on the wall. It moved like a man. But it had a huge head and clawlike hands.

Lambert froze for a minute. Then she stood up and turned around. The alien lifted its head. Slime oozed out of its mouth. **29**

OXYGEN

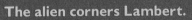
The alien corners Lambert.

Parker stared at the huge alien. It had grown! His weapon was ready, but Lambert was in the line of fire. "Get out of the way!" he screamed at her. "Move!" But Lambert couldn't move. She was cornered. She screamed.

Down the hall, Ripley heard the scream. She dropped Jones's cage and ran toward the sound.

Parker hurled himself at the alien, but it turned and struck him with its powerful tentacles. It lifted him off the ground and

The alien attacks Parker.

squeezed him until blood ran out of his mouth. Then the alien's deadly tongue shot out.

Lambert was too scared to move. She crouched on the floor with her eyes closed. The alien crept toward her and lifted her small body with one tentacle. "No!" Lambert cried. But she was helpless. Her screams echoed through the ship, then died away.

OUNTDOWN

When Ripley reached the shuttle a horrible sight met her. Half of Parker's body was on the floor. The other half hung from a hook on the wall. Lambert was gone, completely consumed by the alien.

Ripley fell back in horror. She was the only one left! Her mind raced. "Blow up the ship," she said out loud, trying to stay calm. "And get to the shuttle." She ran down the halls as fast as she could.

The main control room was full of buttons, switches and levers. She had to think fast.

Ripley flipped a switch, then pulled a giant lever away from the wall. It was heavy and took all her strength to move. Then she loosened four big bolts.

Alarms shrieked. A voice came over the ship's main speaker. "Danger! The ship will self-destruct."

Ripley ran toward the shuttle. The ship was getting hotter by the minute. Steam poured out of the vents and open pipes. Her face was covered with sweat. She looked around. There was no sign of the alien. Then the cat's cage caught her eye.

"Jones!" she cried, grabbing the cage.

At last she saw the shuttle door. She was almost there!

Bursts of fire roared down the hall. The ship was overheating!

"You now have one minute to abandon ship," the voice said.

Ripley could barely breathe. The smoke was choking her. It was **33** now or never. She ran into the shuttle and closed the hatch. Safe! But she still had to take off before the ship blew up.

She strapped herself in and set up the controls. Her fingers fumbled with the switches. She pushed the launch buttons. The shuttle began to detach from the ship.

"The ship will explode in fifteen seconds...fourteen, thirteen, twelve..."

The shuttle took off. It raced through space. Ripley closed her eyes as she saw a blinding light. Then she heard the explosion. The shuttle jolted. Finally everything was still. She sighed. It was over.

 **THE SHUTTLE**

Ripley opened the cat's cage and scooped Jones into her arms. She held him tightly as she looked around the shuttle. She would be in this ship for a long time. The shuttle didn't have enough fuel to make it back to Earth. And it could take years for someone to find her. And maybe they never would.

She set Jones down. It was time to set up the sleeping chamber. As she worked, a tentacle shot out from behind the controls. Ripley gasped and fell back. For a moment she was frozen with fear. But she had to act fast.

She stood up and stumbled to the closet. It was full of space suits. She waited, watching the alien as it emerged from behind the control board.

The creature opened its mouth. The white tongue slid out. Globs of clear slime dripped to the floor. It was waiting.

Ripley looked around her. What was she going to do? Ash had said the alien was impossible to kill.

An idea came to her. She stepped into a space suit. First one leg, then the other. She zipped it up slowly, watching the alien the **34** whole time.

Only Ripley and Jones are left.

Ripley steps from the closet.

Then she pulled out a helmet and placed it on her head. Now she would be safe from any changes in cabin pressure. She grabbed a weapon and stepped from the closet.

Ripley sat down at the control panel and strapped herself in. Then she began to press buttons. Steam shot out of the vents above the control panel. She wanted the steam to hit the alien. But she had to find the right button.

Finally she hit it. A piercing scream echoed through the shuttle. The alien squirmed.

36   Ripley stared in horror. She had to stay calm so she could open the hatch. She was safely strapped in, but the alien wasn't.

Ripley closed her eyes. She needed to wait until the right moment. This was her only chance. She counted to three and opened her eyes. The alien stood ready to strike.

Screaming, Ripley pushed the button. The hatch shot open. A

The alien is sucked to the shuttle door.

powerful vacuum sucked the alien to the door. But the creature clung to the ship. Ripley raised her gun and fired, hitting the alien's chest. Finally it fell into space. As soon as it was gone she dropped the weapon and closed the hatch.

Ripley watched the alien's body fall through space until it

disappeared. When the ship was pressurized again, she unbuckled herself and took off the space suit.

With a sigh she pressed the buttons on the control panel to set up the sleeping chamber. Then Ripley and Jones curled up for their long ride through space.

Ripley watches the alien fall through space.

The makers of *Alien* prey on our fear of the unknown.

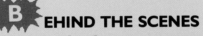EHIND THE SCENES

Since *Alien* was released, the monster in the title role has become famous. Why is this creature so frightening?

In this case the filmmakers prey on our fear of the unknown. If the ship's crew had known what they were dealing with, they wouldn't have been so scared. But every time they saw the alien it was different. It looked different. It used different ways to kill them. The alien kept changing.

Many creatures in nature go through marked changes. Frogs and some insects change in remarkable ways. This change is called metamorphosis.

A tadpole is a swimming creature. It has a round body, a long tail and gills. As it grows the tail disappears. The creature grows arms, legs and lungs. When it is fully grown, it is a frog. A frog is able to live on land and in the water.

Some insects go through a similar change. A butterfly begins as an egg. When the egg hatches, out crawls a caterpillar. Then the wormlike caterpillar weaves a cocoon around itself. Inside the cocoon, it continues to grow. When it finally comes out, the creature is a butterfly. At this stage the insect is an adult. It won't change anymore. But the alien never stops changing!

The alien starts off as an egg on the strange planet. The next time we see the creature it is covering Kane's face. In this stage it looks like a sea creature. It has a hard shell like a crab. And it has tentacles like an octopus.

When the alien bursts from Kane's chest, it resembles a snake. Then it begins to molt, just like a real snake. When a snake sheds its skin, it is said to "molt." The skin peels off because the snake's body is growing and the old skin is too tight. When Brett finds the shed skin, we know that the alien is growing. And it keeps growing.

The changing alien is metamorphosis gone wild! The film's creators built on a fact of nature to create a terrifying tale.

MODEL MANIA

Director Ridley Scott wanted the special effects for *Alien* to be just right. So he hired people to make models of nearly every object filmed. They built a model of each alien form. They even built a model of the planet.

Some models were small. Others were life-size and showed every detail. It took the model makers about a year to complete their work. It took so long because the models were constantly being changed. At times Scott would throw away a model and send the artists back to the drawing board for a brand-new idea.

Three different models of the spaceship were made. The biggest model measured 18 feet and weighed 800 pounds! This model changed color three times.

 GIANT PLANET?

The alien landscape where the spaceship lands looks realistic. That's because a life-size surface of the planet was designed and built. This was possible because the studio where *Alien* was filmed was so big. Most of the filming was done in a huge warehouse in England.

Scott made the landscape look even bigger by using tiny people to film some of the exploration scenes. Scott's children played the crew in the suits! This was easy to do. In the faraway shots the children's faces were hidden by their space helmets. In the close-up scenes adult actors were used.

Children play the crew in the exploration scenes.

Special space suits were designed for these scenes. But the designers forgot one thing: There was no way for the actors to breathe inside the suits! The adult actors felt weak and dizzy if they wore the suits for long.

This made filming the exploration scenes difficult. When the adult actors complained, they were ignored! Nobody believed that the suits were hard to work in. It wasn't until one of Ridley Scott's children actually fainted that the problem was corrected.

AN OR DUMMY?

One of the scariest scenes in *Alien* is the one in which the creature bursts from Kane's chest. For this scene a fake body was made. Most of what we see is this dummy. Only the head and arms are really actor John Hurt.

Only the head and arms belong to actor John Hurt.

First John Hurt was "installed" in the galley table. The table had been cut into sections. Then it was put together around him. His head and arms were above the table. But the rest of his body was hidden underneath.

Then came the hard part. The fake body had to be positioned just right. It had to look real. It had to be connected to the actor's head and shoulders. And the alien creature below had to be in the right position to pop out. It took an entire morning to set up this scene.

ECRETS

The "chest-burster" alien was created just for this scene. Its design was a well-guarded secret. All work was done behind closed doors. Even the studio executives were kept in the dark.

Director Ridley Scott wanted this scene to be shocking. So he decided to try the element of surprise—even on the actors. No one saw the alien until it burst out of Kane's chest.

The surprise worked! The cast was truly disgusted.

Before filming the scene, the actress playing Lambert was warned that she would be squirted with some fake blood. But so much blood shot out from the mechanical chest that she was knocked off her feet!

UPPET SHOW

The "chest-burster" itself was actually a hand puppet. It was made from a plaster mold. Special gills and a tiny air bag that moved up and down inside the puppet were installed to make it "breathe." To make it look like the giant alien, metal teeth were molded and snapped into the mouth.

The puppet came to life with the help of Roger Dicken, the man who created it. Dicken made the creature pop out of Kane's chest **45**

and turn as it looked at the crew. Other technicians operated the creature's gills and chest.

To film the alien's exit shot, the dinner table was cut in half. A special trolley was built for Dicken to lie down on. He slid along underneath the table while working the puppet on the tabletop.

UIT UP

The giant alien was actually a carefully constructed costume. Inside the suit was actor Bolaji Badejo, who is a giant himself. He is six feet ten inches tall!

To be sure that the suit would fit Badejo, a whole-body cast was taken of the actor. A man named H. R. Giger made a statue from

The alien suit was so hot it could only be worn for a few minutes.

the cast. Tubes, bones and other objects were attached to the statue. Then another mold was taken of this shape. Upon this mold the final alien suit was built. Giger used some unusual materials for his creation: polyester, rubber, animal meat, real bones and oysters!

The costume had more than ten separate sections. Putting it on was an ordeal. It took over an hour for Badejo to suit up. Once in it the actor could wear it for only ten to fifteen minutes because it was so hot. He said that wearing the alien head was like having your head stuck in a giant banana!

MAZING HEADS

Three different heads were made for the giant alien. They were all molded out of clay and then cast with fiberglass and soft polyurethane. But only one of the heads was designed to make all the creature's movements.

On this supermodel the moving parts were attached with interlocking joints. These joints worked together. When one part moved, the attached parts moved too. A bicycle chain has the same kind of joints. If you move one link the others move with it. The monster's face, jaws and tongue were all connected with interlocking joints.

The tongue moved in and out of the mouth on a geared track. The track was shifted with levers. The levers worked like the gear shifter on a bicycle: When you click one into place, the gear changes.

The tongue also had a special spring. It could be coiled up and held in, or let loose. Springing it loose worked well for quick movements.

The whole tongue was coated with special chemicals. This made the slime look oozy and last longer. The longer the ooze lasted, the more scenes they could shoot in a row.